THE SECRET EXPLORERS

AND THE HAUNTED CASTLE

CONTENTS

Chapter One
JOURNEY TO THE PAST

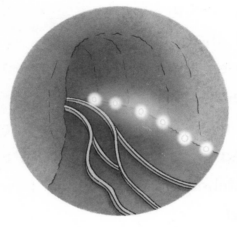

"Hey, look at these old mining tools," Gustavo said to his little brother, Adriano. "They could be 300 years old!"

Adriano was more interested in following the rail tracks that led into another tunnel.

Gustavo and his family were touring an

old gold mine at Ouro Preto, in Brazil. It was a long way from their home in Rio de Janeiro. Gustavo had spent the journey reading about Ouro Preto's past. He learned that when gold was discovered there, people rushed to get rich and it became the busiest city in Latin America.

A wailing noise echoed through the mine. Adriano bounded to Gustavo's side and clutched his hand. "What was that?" he asked.

"It was probably wind whistling through the tunnels," Gustavo replied.

The tour guide asked, "Did anyone hear that?" Several people nodded.

"I did," whispered Adriano.

The guide said, "There are rumors... No, I'd better not say."

"Oh, tell us!" said a woman.

The guide spoke in a low voice. "There are rumors that some of the tunnels are haunted by ghosts... The ghosts of miners!"

Gustavo, standing to one side, saw the guide's hand flick toward the wall. The next moment, the lights went out and the tunnel was plunged into darkness. People yelped in surprise. It was so black that Gustavo saw no difference if he opened or closed his eyes.

He squeezed Adriano's hand. "It's just the guide playing a trick," he said.

When the lights came back on, Gustavo's dad looked across and raised his eyebrows as if to ask, "Okay?"

Gustavo nodded, then grinned at Adriano. "That was scary!" he said. "Did you feel shaky when it went dark? I did!"

His brother smiled. "Yes, but it was fun!"

Gustavo agreed. He'd read stories about ghostly shipwrecks and castles. Some parts of the stories were true, but he knew that the ghostly parts had been added to make the tales more exciting.

"Let's get a snack," Adriano said, and trotted over to their mom. Gustavo was about to follow him when he noticed something glowing on the rocky wall in a side tunnel.

Was it a nugget of gold that the miners had missed? When he looked closer, his heart leapt. This was something far more exciting than gold! It was a glowing symbol of a compass.

Gustavo was one of eight children from across the world with matching compass badges. They were the Secret Explorers. Each one was an expert in a different subject, and they used their knowledge to solve problems. Gustavo was their History expert.

"A new mission's waiting for us," Gustavo whispered. "A new adventure!"

With a crackling sound, a door appeared in the solid rock. Gustavo glanced over to his family, who were busy choosing snacks from the selection in Dad's backpack. Gustavo knew that no time at all would pass while he was away, so they wouldn't miss him.

He pushed the door open and stepped forward into brilliant white light. A strong wind swirled around him. Then the light faded to reveal the Secret Explorers' headquarters—the Exploration Station.

He was the first Explorer to arrive. "Gustavo, here!" he said aloud.

Eight computers were ranged along a gleaming stone wall. Comfy armchairs and squishy sofas stood in front of displays of objects collected by the Explorers on their missions. In the middle of the floor was a huge map of the world. An image of the Milky Way covered the ceiling.

"Roshni, here!" said a voice. Gustavo turned to see a girl with a long braid come through the glowing doorway. She had a faint red ring around one eye.

Gustavo grinned. "You've been pressing too hard against your telescope!" Roshni laughed and nodded. She was the Space Explorer.

The Marine Life Explorer was next to arrive. "Connor, here!" he said. His jeans were damp around the bottoms. Gustavo guessed Connor had been on the beach.

Two more Explorers arrived almost at once. "Tamiko, here!" said the first. Her shiny hair was held in place by a silver dinosaur barrette. Tamiko was the Dinosaur Explorer.

"Cheng, here!" said the second Explorer. He was the Geology expert. Gustavo thought anyone could guess that by Cheng's bulging pockets. They were usually stuffed with pieces of rock.

Next was a tall girl in a cycling helmet on. She saluted smartly. "Leah, here!" she said. Leah was the Biology Explorer.

"Kiki, here!" said the Engineering Explorer. She had two wrenches and a screwdriver tucked in her top pocket.

Last to come through the door was the Rainforest Explorer, with his huge backpack. "Ollie, here!" he said.

The Secret Explorers gathered around the world map on the floor.

"Where will the mission be?" said Tamiko. "Any guesses?"

"The Antarctic!" said Leah.

"The Gobi Desert!" Cheng suggested.

"A coral island," said Connor.

Then Kiki said, "Sshh! Look!"

A light had appeared on the map.

"That's somewhere in Central Europe," said Ollie.

A beam of light rose from the map. It

opened out into a screen that showed a huge castle on top of a hill. Towers and turrets overlooked the countryside, and its tall walls seemed to grow out of solid rock.

That's a Medieval castle, thought Gustavo. His mind filled with images of knights and jousts and battles. I hope the Exploration Station chooses me for this mission!

The Explorers gasped as a strange green light appeared beside the castle. It drifted around the walls, then vanished.

"What was that?" Cheng wondered.

"I don't know," said Gustavo. "It must be something to do with the mission."

Tamiko pointed at him. "You're about to find out," she said with a grin. "You've been chosen for the mission!"

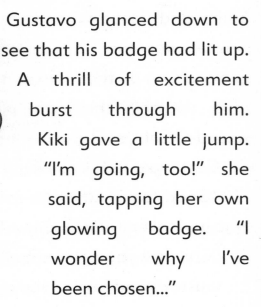

Gustavo glanced down to see that his badge had lit up. A thrill of excitement burst through him. Kiki gave a little jump. "I'm going, too!" she said, tapping her own glowing badge. "I wonder why I've been chosen..."

"You're the Engineering expert," said Connor. "So maybe the castle portcullis is broken. Or the dungeons might be flooded. We know the Exploration Station always chooses the right Explorers for a mission."

Roshni pressed a big red button on the wall. The world map seemed to dissolve, and up through the floor rose a rickety old go-kart. It didn't look like much, with its peeling paint and rusty wheels. But this scruffy vehicle was the Beagle, and it took the Explorers on all their missions. It was named after the ship that carried the Victorian scientist, Charles Darwin.

Gustavo and Kiki climbed into the seats.

"Good luck!" called the other Explorers, who had taken their places at the computers.

"Call us if you need help," said Ollie.

Gustavo and Kiki waved goodbye to their

friends, then zoomed off into dazzling white light. Wind roared past their ears.

"The Beagle's shakier than usual!" shouted Kiki.

"It feels like we're driving across bumpy ground!" said Gustavo. His voice wobbled with every thump.

When the light faded, he found they were sitting on the front bench of a cart, which was being pulled by a horse—and Gustavo was holding the reins!

"Where are we?" wondered Kiki.

All around them were hills and forests. They were on a track that wound up through the trees. Ahead of them were lots of other carts, trundling forward in a long line. Gustavo glanced around to see more carts behind them too.

The carts were all stacked with goods

and the drivers wore strange clothes, like tunics and leggings. Gustavo and Kiki's clothes had transformed, too—instead of their jeans and t-shirts, they were wearing sleeveless tops over tunics, with thin pants tucked into leather boots.

Gustavo gasped. "Look—up there!"

At the top of the hill they were climbing was a castle—the one the Exploration Station had shown them. It was very tall, with stone walls and lots of towers. Flags fluttered from the battlements.

"That must be where we're heading," Gustavo said.

"I like the towers with the pointed roofs," said Kiki. "They remind me of headdresses ladies wore in the olden days."

Gustavo shivered with excitement. *That's a Medieval castle*, he thought.

And we're wearing Medieval clothes...

"Kiki," he said. "This is the Medieval Era."

She stared. "You mean we're in the olden days?"

Gustavo grinned happily. "The very olden days— we've gone 500 years back in time!"

Chapter Two
A MEDIEVAL MYSTERY

"Okay," Kiki said. She took a deep breath. "We've gone back in time to the Medieval Era, and we're on our way to a castle. But where's the Beagle?"

The old go-kart usually changed into a form of transportation to help the Explorers on their mission. It had been a dune buggy, a helicopter, and even a submarine.

"We can't manage without the Beagle," Kiki said anxiously. "We won't be able to contact the Exploration Station."

BEEP BIP BEEP!

Gustavo grinned. "This cart must be the Beagle!"

"Whew!" said Kiki.

BEEEP!

Gustavo passed Kiki the reins and jumped into the back of the cart. He crouched down and felt around a panel at the back. He pulled it away. "Ta-da!"

Inside was a computer and all the tech gadgets they were used to.

Kiki grinned. "Smart Beagle!"

BEEP BEEP!

They both laughed at the Beagle's polite "thank you."

Gustavo searched the cart. He found a wooden trunk beneath some burlap material. When he opened it, he saw that it was packed with swords, arrows, and long wooden spears with metal tips.

"These are lances," he said. "They must belong to a knight."

He glanced at the sleeveless tops he and Kiki were wearing over their tunics.

"These tabards are in the livery of a knight," he said. "I think we must be squires."

"Liver what?" said Kiki.

"Livery," said Gustavo. "It's like a uniform in the knight's colors, with his symbol on the front. A squire wears his knight's livery."

"Or her knight's livery," said Kiki.

"Er, these are different times," Gustavo said. "Women weren't allowed to do some jobs."

"Huh! Like being a squire or a knight, I suppose," said Kiki. "How unfair!"

Gustavo nodded. "Squires are trainee knights, so you should probably pretend to be a boy. Otherwise, you'll end up doing something else—and I won't be able to complete the mission on my own."

BEEPBEEPBEEP!

Gustavo laughed. "Well, on my own apart from the Beagle! Though I'd look funny getting my knight ready for battle with the help of a cart."

"B-b-battle?" Kiki said.

"Probably just a tournament," Gustavo said hastily, "with jousting on horseback. That could be why all these carts are going to the castle. For a tournament they'll need food for hundreds of people, and tents for the crowds, and extra stablehands to look after the horses."

Their horse whinnied as they followed the track around a corner. The castle was very close now, looming over them.

Kiki passed the reins back to Gustavo and stuffed her hair under a hat she found nearby as a disguise. "There. I'd better use a boy's name, too. What's a Medieval-sounding name?"

"How about Geoffrey, after Geoffrey Chaucer?" suggested Gustavo. "He was a Medieval writer."

Ahead was a large, gilded carriage. It gleamed golden where the sun struck it. Soldiers on horseback rode beside it.

"That carriage must belong to someone powerful," Gustavo said. He drew a sharp breath.

"What is it?" Kiki asked.

"Central Europe was ruled by an emperor in Medieval times," said Gustavo. "Maybe that's his carriage!"

They were almost at the castle now. There was a moat around it, with a drawbridge that lay over the water. Guards were stopping each cart when they reached the drawbridge. They asked the drivers questions and searched the carts before letting them cross. Soon it was the Beagle's turn.

A guard checked under the sacking. Gustavo held his breath. *Will he spot the Beagle's electronics?* he wondered. *What if he guesses we're from the future?* But the guard flung the burlap material down, saying, "Keep moving, lads."

Kiki giggled. "First time I've been called a lad!"

Their horse pulled the Beagle over the wooden drawbridge. Gustavo looked up as they passed beneath a gate made of wood and metal, raised up above the entrance. "That's the portcullis," he said. "It can be dropped to stop enemies from coming in."

They drove into a large courtyard. The main castle entrance was straight ahead, with towers on each side. Workshops and stables lined the courtyard, and delicious cooking smells wafted from a big stone building on the left. Carts were being parked on the right, near where a small chapel nestled in a corner.

The golden carriage had stopped in the middle of the courtyard. Lots of people had gathered around it, including a tall man in a long blue cloak fringed with fur and a lady in a green gown.

A servant unhitched the Explorers' horse and led it toward the stables. Gustavo and Kiki jumped down to join the crowd. Beside them was a woman with rough red hands, wearing a long brown dress.

"Excuse me," Gustavo asked her, pointing to the couple by the carriage. "Who are they?"

"That's the lord and lady of the castle, Count Maximilian and Countess Cornelia. Don't they look grand? I'm Margrit, their personal washerwoman," she added proudly. "Oh, my—look!"

The crowd gasped as a man stepped out of the golden carriage. His jeweled silk hat sparkled and flashed in the sunshine, and his scarlet cloak was thickly embroidered with gold thread.

"He looks so rich," breathed Kiki. "Is he the Emperor, Margrit?"

"Nay, lad," she

replied. "That's his brother, Prince Alfred."

A voice bellowed, "Make way for His Highness!" The crowd scurried out of the Prince's way.

A man with a leather apron headed toward Margrit. "I've got the latest news from the prince's servants," he said to her. "They say the Emperor has argued with Count Maximilian. They think the Emperor will take away the castle to punish him—and give it to Prince Alfred!"

"Oh, Otto, no!" said Margrit. "We don't want him here!"

"That sounds like bad news," said Gustavo. "Will you lose your jobs?"

Margrit folded her arms. "Probably not. But our Count's a good man. Prince Alfred's unkind and cruel. I can't bear to think of him being in charge."

As the nobles went indoors, the crowd melted away.

"Let's find out where the squires are supposed to go," said Gustavo to Kiki.

But before they could set off, a terrified shriek echoed around the courtyard.

"AAAAARGH!"

Gustavo felt the hairs on the back of his neck stand up.

A soldier burst from an arched doorway beside the chapel. He was white-faced and shaking. Otto ran to stop him falling down.

"Ghost!" he wailed. "A g-g-ghost... in the crypt!"

Startled faces looked out from the kitchen and workshops. A frightened dairymaid gave a scream.

As another soldier ordered everyone back to work, Gustavo pulled Kiki aside. "I don't believe in ghosts," he said quietly. "So what could have frightened him so much?"

"I don't believe in ghosts, either," said Kiki. "But something in there spooked him. The crypt must be quite creepy—it's where they bury people in tombs, isn't it?"

"Oi!" the soldiers called. "Go away, lads."

"Yes, sir," said Gustavo. "Come along, Ki...er, I mean...Geoffrey."

They walked away slowly. Once the soldier was out of sight, Gustavo said, "Let's sneak back and look inside that crypt. There must be a logical explanation for what the guard saw."

They hurried through the arched doorway of the chapel. A set of stone stairs led downward. All along the passage were footprints in the dust.

And they were glowing. Glowing green!

Kiki gasped. "Remember the green light on the screen at the Exploration Station? This must have something to do with our mission!"

Gustavo nodded. "It's up to us to solve the mystery of these spooky footprints!"

Chapter Three
A SCARY STORY

When Gustavo and Kiki left the crypt, they found several frightened-looking workers huddled in the courtyard.

"Surely they don't believe there's a ghost?" said Kiki.

Gustavo shrugged. "They might," he said. "Medieval people were superstitious.

They didn't have scientific explanations for weird things. But we'll find the explanation for those footprints."

"Yes, we'll look for clues to help us figure it out," said Kiki. "Do you think squires are supposed to go to the stables?"

They went to find out. Small boys ran to and from the stables with buckets of water, and the Explorers found older boys grooming powerful-looking horses.

The Stable Master looked at Gustavo and Kiki. "Ah, so you're the new squires to Sir Leonard. This huge beast is your responsibility," he said, stroking a glossy black horse. "He's called Tiber. Now go and eat—Tiber will wake you in the morning, ready for the tournament."

Gustavo asked, "Where do we sleep?"

The man grinned. "With Tiber, of course!

How else will he wake you up? Besides, you don't want him stolen in the night, do you? Sir Leonard would be furious. And so would Prince Alfred, because Sir Leonard is his best knight—Prince Alfred gets the glory if Sir Leonard wins the tournament."

Gustavo and Kiki exchanged a glance. "I'm not sure I want anything to do with Prince Alfred or his knight," muttered Kiki.

The Explorers filled Tiber's trough with oats. The big horse ate hungrily.

A freckle-faced boy was crouched in the stable doorway, feeding strong-smelling fish to a dusty gray cat. He glanced at Gustavo and Kiki. "Tom caught nineteen mice today," he said proudly.

"Great," said Gustavo. "Er, where can Geoffrey and I get some food too?"

"The other squires have already eaten the stew," said the boy. "But I'll get you some cheese and fresh bread from the kitchen."

"Thank you," said Kiki and Gustavo.

Soon they were strolling around the courtyard, enjoying the bread and tasty cheese and keeping an eye out for any clues about the green footprints. People were carrying hay for horses, wine for the nobles, ale for the guards, and flags and bunting for tomorrow's tournament.

A man rolled a barrel toward them. The words *"BLACK POWDER"* were painted on it.

"Out of the way, squires! I don't want to blow you up!" The man winked as they leapt clear of it. He rolled the barrel toward the armory, where a row of cannons were being cleaned.

"What's 'black powder'?" Kiki wondered.

"It's like gunpowder," said Gustavo, "but it creates a lot of smoke."

A voice from the kitchen door shouted over. "Squires! Help needed! Go to the storehouse and collect supplies for the welcome feast!"

Gustavo and Kiki hurried off and collected a sack of flour each, which they carried on their backs and staggered across the courtyard and into the kitchen.

The kitchen was hot! And noisy! Women were stirring, chopping, slicing, kneading, mixing, and shouting to each other over hissing steam and bubbling pots. Huge joints of meat hung in a massive fireplace, being turned slowly on spits by small boys and girls. Gustavo and Kiki dumped their sacks and went for the next bunch of supplies. When they'd finished, they helped themselves to cups of cool water from the bucket at the top of a nearby well.

"What could have been making those footprints glow green?" wondered Kiki. "When everyone's at the feast, we can do some investigating."

A voice behind them snapped, "You two!"

A well-dressed servant was calling from a doorway. "Go up to the Great Hall," he said. "The feast has already begun."

"But we don't work in the kitchen, we're squires—"

"I don't care," said the servant. "Everyone helps on feast days."

Kiki sighed. "No investigating for us, then..."

As they climbed a stone spiral staircase, Gustavo said, "Did you know that stairs inside castles always turn clockwise?"

"Why's that?" asked Kiki.

"So an enemy climbing up with his sword

in his right hand would find it hard to swing it at anyone above him," Gustavo said. He could still hardly believe he was in a Medieval castle, in the Medieval era! "I can hear music," he said. "We're nearly at the feast."

The top of the stairs opened onto a room with tables against the walls. Young men were carrying lots of dishes through a curtained doorway.

"Take these," said a red-haired man, thrusting jugs of wine at Gustavo and Kiki. "Make sure the guests' goblets are never empty. You're serving the high table."

"Sir, which is the high table?" asked Kiki.

"It's the one on the platform. High table, get it?" said the man. "Go!"

They hurried through the curtain into a vast hall with a lofty roof. Long tables were laden with dishes of roast meats, fish, pies, and fruit tarts, with people seated all around them. The air was filled with laughter, talk, and shouts, while in a gallery above them musicians played stringed instruments that Gustavo knew were called lutes. Seated at the high table were Prince Alfred, Count Maximilian, Countess Cornelia, and the other nobles.

"Ah, more wine!" said the Count, smiling

at Gustavo. He and Kiki started filling up the nobles' silver goblets.

Countess Cornelia smiled too. "Thank you," she said, when Gustavo served her. "Do make sure you help yourself to some of the desserts, won't you? The cakes are delicious."

Gustavo was thinking how nice she was, when a high, whiny voice said, "Boy! Wine! Here! Now!"

It was Prince Alfred. Gustavo hurried to fill his goblet. As he did so, he saw the much fancier food on the top table, including a towering dessert that was an exact copy of the castle, with touches of gold on the turrets. Gustavo thought it was made of sugar, which he knew was very expensive in medieval times.

"Stop staring, boy and fill my goblet again," Alfred whined. He turned to the count.

"Maximilian, wasn't it funny when your peasants were scared by a ghost in your crypt?" He laughed nastily. "Silly fools! In the city, people aren't taken in by such nonsense." Alfred leaned back in his chair and tossed a grape into his mouth. "I like this castle, Maximilian. If I lived here, I'd teach your peasants a thing or two about how to behave." He smiled, but Gustavo thought his eyes looked as cold as ice. "Maybe I will be living here one day..."

The Count frowned. "Prince Alfred," he said. "Let me tell you a story."

"Make it good," said the Prince. "I get bored easily."

The Count began, "There was once a battle..."

Gustavo moved closer so he could overhear. Close by, Kiki pretended to fill up more goblets, so she could listen to the story too.

"A battle just beyond this castle," the Count continued. "My grandfather wished to honor the brave men who died, so he buried one knight in a grand tomb in our crypt. He was known as the Horned Knight

because his battle helmet had two horns."

The Prince grunted. "So?"

"Today," said the Count, "after the report of a ghost, our crypt was searched. The Horned Knight's tomb was open. It was empty."

The Prince turned pale. "You mean the Horned Knight..."

Count Maximilian nodded. "He was the ghost."

Gustavo and Kiki stared at each other. Gustavo knew they were both thinking the same thing. *If there's no such thing as ghosts—what really happened?*

Chapter Four
THE HORNED KNIGHT

Kiki was snoring by the time Gustavo reached his straw pallet in the stable. Tiber the horse was snoozing gently.

When the nobles had gone to bed, the guests had continued feasting. Gustavo had been kept behind, and ordered to fetch this and fetch that, sweep here and sweep there.

All he had really wanted to do was investigate the story of the Horned Knight!

Historians need evidence to figure out what happened in the past, Gustavo thought. *So I need to find evidence to solve the mystery of the ghost...*

He shook Kiki. "Wake up," he whispered. "Let's go to the crypt and investigate."

Kiki followed him out of the stable. Gustavo took a flaming torch from the wall outside. Mist swirled around the courtyard as they crossed to the chapel's arched entrance.

Once inside, they crept down the stone staircase. The glowing footprints had disappeared.

At the bottom, the chilly air smelled musty. It was pitch dark outside the pool of torchlight, and the flickering flames seemed to make the shadows dance.

Gustavo held the torch high. They saw several big, carved tombs.

"The Count's ancestors must be buried in those," said Gustavo. He moved past them and found a great tomb with a carved stone helmet on top. A helmet with two horns...

"Kiki!" he said, "this must be the Horned Knight's tomb."

"It can't be," she said. "It isn't open." She peered at it. "It's not even been touched—these thick cobwebs must have been here for years."

"You're right." Gustavo ran his hand over the top. "It's even got lichen growing on it. This tomb has never been disturbed."

They returned to the courtyard, where the mist had thickened.

Gustavo said, "So the Count was lying to Prince Alfred when he said the Horned Knight's tomb was open." He returned the torch to its holder on the wall. "But why? Why would he tell him about the ghost of the Horned Knight?"

A terrible shriek tore through the air.

The Explorers jumped.

"What was that?" said Gustavo.

"It came from the tower where the Prince is staying," said Kiki, her eyes wide.

"How do you know where he's staying?"

Kiki pointed to a flag flying over the left-hand tower. It had the two-headed eagle symbol on it.

"Of course!" said Gustavo. "Let's investi–"

He stopped as more ghastly screams rang out. At the foot of the Prince's tower, soldiers were bumping into each other as they dashed around in the mist. They didn't seem to know what to do or where to go.

One soldier, clutching his sword, said to his officer, "Sir, we don't know what's going on. No intruder has gotten into that tower, so the Prince is safe. I've been by the entrance all night."

The officer shook his head. "You probably fell asleep," he growled, before charging around, trying to calm the rest of his men.

Gustavo and Kiki stepped back until they were hidden by the mist. They kept close to the Prince's tower wall, away from the chaos in the courtyard. Nobody saw them slip inside.

They hurried up a spiral staircase and reached a landing. On one side was a big wooden door with a gold handle. "The Prince's room?" Gustavo whispered.

They froze as clanging noises echoed ahead of them. It sounded as if someone was banging pots together.

A figure appeared at the corridor's far end. It clomped along the corridor with slow, heavy steps. The Explorers pressed themselves back into a dark alcove. When Gustavo peered out, he saw the figure was a knight in armor, with a visor covering its face. And it was glowing green!

Gustavo swallowed. "Its helmet has horns," he whispered to Kiki.

"It's the Horned Knight!" she whispered back.

They huddled together in the alcove, trembling, as the Horned Knight passed. It stopped outside the Prince's room and rattled the doorknob.

"Go away!" shrieked the Prince from inside his room. "I don't believe in ghosts—this is just a silly prank! Get lost!" But his voice was shaking with fright.

The Horned Knight rattled the door one more time. Then it turned, and walked back the way it had come.

Gustavo and Kiki clutched each other's hands. Once the knight had gone past them, they peered out and watched it go. Then, before their eyes, the Horned Knight simply vanished.

One moment it was there—and the next, it was gone.

Gustavo realized he'd been holding his breath. "What just happened?" he said.

"I don't know," Kiki said in a wobbly voice. "But there's got to be a logical explanation. Isn't there?"

Gustavo nodded. "We don't believe in ghosts, and we don't believe in glowing ghosts, and we definitely don't believe in disappearing glowing ghosts. Do we?"

As they started back down the spiral staircase, Gustavo felt his fright melt away. They would solve this mystery!

"Kiki," he said, "do you think the Horned Knight is trying to scare the Prince into leaving?"

Kiki nodded. "Nobody wants him to take over the castle. Especially not—"

Gustavo stopped on the last step. "Especially not the Count. Kiki, Count Maximilian was the one who made up the ghost story. Could he be pretending to be the Horned Knight?"

Chapter Five
TIBER'S FRIGHT

After just two hours of sleep, Gustavo could hardly open his eyes when he heard Tiber whinnying. He sat up and poked Kiki. "Wake up," he said. "We need to investigate whether the Count is the Horned—"

"Can't," Kiki mumbled sleepily. "It's tournament day."

The other squires and stable boys were stirring. Gustavo went to fetch water for Tiber while Kiki gave him a good brush.

"I'm glad you know about horses, Kiki," Gustavo said as he returned with the water. "Otherwise no one would believe we were squires."

"I don't know that much," she replied, "but I help take care of my cousins' ponies sometimes, so I know a bit. But really I'm just copying the others." She fixed a metal plate over Tiber's face. "This must be to protect him from lances. Pass that cloth coat thing. It goes on before the saddle."

Gustavo helped arrange the cloth over Tiber's back and head. "I've read about these," he said. "It's called a caparison. Sometimes they stuff straw inside to protect the horses."

"Nobody else is doing that," said Kiki, glancing around. "Maybe this competition is a friendly one, so no one will get hurt," she suggested. "Hey, the caparison has our double-headed eagle on it. Everyone will know that Sir Leonard is the Prince's champion."

Once Tiber was ready, the Stable Master said, "Time to break your fast, lads."

"Break our what?" said Kiki.

Gustavo giggled. "He means eat breakfast."

Outside, the courtyard was busier than ever, with workers dashing around and yelling to one another. The Explorers got bread, slices of ham, and pickled onions from the kitchen, and Kiki took two rosy apples from a barrel by the door.

People were going in and out of a

small gate that led out of the courtyard. Squires were taking the horses through there, too. "Better get moving!" he yelled.

Gustavo and Kiki ran to the stable. Tiber was tossing his head, looking restless.

"Come on, boy," Kiki said. "You're excited, aren't you?"

She led Tiber out, and Gustavo followed her into the courtyard and through the gate. They crossed a bridge that had been laid over the moat and walked around behind the castle.

Brightly colored circular tents had been set up. There was a grandstand with seats for the nobles, and three chairs, like thrones, in the front.

"Those fancy seats will be for the Prince and the Count and Countess," said Gustavo.

"Doesn't everything look fantastic with all the flags waving above the grandstand?" said Kiki. "And all the lords and ladies are taking their seats. They look wonderful, all dressed up!"

A long rail ran the length of the jousting run. Gustavo explained that the knights would start at opposite ends, one on each side. "They charge at each other and score points for hitting their opponent with the lance," he said. "If they knock their opponent off his horse, they win."

Kiki nudged Gustavo. "The important guests are coming," she said, as the tall figure of the Count in his cloak, and the Countess in a blue dress, made their way to the grandstand. The Count waved at the crowd.

Is he really pretending to be the Horned Knight? wondered Gustavo.

Next came Prince Alfred. Everyone bowed or curtsied to the Prince, but he walked by without a glance.

"He looks as if he's got a smell under his nose," said Kiki.

Two ladies-in-waiting followed, muttering quietly.

"So rude," Gustavo heard one of the ladies say.

"He doesn't deserve the title of Prince," said the other. "Our Count and Countess are far more gracious than him."

Gustavo pointed to where the horses and riders were gathered. "Let's fetch Tiber and find Sir Leonard," he said.

As they threaded their way between the tents, Gustavo felt uneasy. Servants and grooms were muttering about the screams they had heard from the Prince's tower, and how they'd hardly slept for fear of the ghost of the Horned Knight.

"Where have you two been?" said a sharp voice. An armored knight, carrying a shield with the double-headed eagle, glared at them. A smug-faced squire was giving the armor a final shine.

"That must be Sir Leonard," muttered Kiki. "He looks as unfriendly as his master, the Prince."

"Sorry, Sir Leonard," said Gustavo. "We were—"

"No excuses!" the knight snapped. "Bring that horse here."

Kiki led Tiber over, and the smug squire helped Sir Leonard mount. As the knight sat down heavily on the saddle, Tiber squealed and bucked. He rose up on his hind legs—and Sir Leonard went flying. The knight landed on the ground with an almighty crash.

Tiber bolted, chased by grooms, while Gustavo and Kiki stood open-mouthed.

The smug squire helped Sir Leonard up. He took off his helmet to reveal a face purple with rage. "What— what—?" Sir Leonard spluttered.

"Tiber's never done anything like that before," said his smug squire.

The Prince was rushing over with his servants.

"What happened?" he asked Sir Leonard. "Is it this rough ground? Is it too crowded? It's absolute chaos! No wonder your horse bucked. These people don't know how to stage a joust properly!" His face turned red. "This castle is a disgrace!" he barked, looking around. "All you peasants and servants need a strong master to whip you into shape. I'm going to tell my brother the Emperor to give the castle to me!"

In the horrified silence that followed, one brave young squire spoke. "Perhaps Tiber saw the ghost," he said.

"Nonsense," said Prince Alfred, but he had turned pale.

Tiber was brought back by the grooms who had caught him. His ears were flat and he was tossing his head. Kiki took the reins and spoke gently to him. "Easy, boy."

Everyone was muttering about the ghost. They stopped when Count Maximilian came over and called for calm. "Please get ready for the next joust," he said, then turned to the Prince. "Don't worry, I'll loan Sir Leonard one of my horses. Do come and watch the tournament, Your Highness."

"Are you jousting, Maximilian?" Prince Alfred asked, grumpily.

The Count shook his head and laughed. "Oh no," he said. "My days in armor are over."

Gustavo caught Kiki's eye. "I don't think that's true," he whispered.

The two Explorers walked Tiber back to the stables. When Kiki unsaddled him, something fell out from underneath it. Gustavo picked it up. It was a pair of blue leather gloves, rolled into a ball.

"They're lady's gloves, by the size of

them," said Kiki.

"So this is what startled Tiber," Gustavo said. "When Sir Leonard sat on the saddle, the gloves pressed onto Tiber's back and startled him."

Kiki laid her face against the horse's side. "Poor Tiber," she said.

"A ghost isn't to blame," Gustavo said. "Nor a curse. Count Maximilian's behind this. He shouldn't have upset Tiber. But who can blame him for trying to stop the Prince getting the castle?"

"It didn't worked though, did it?" said Kiki. "Now Prince Alfred is determined to take the castle."

Gustavo frowned thoughtfully. "Maybe we're not here just to prove there isn't a ghost. Kiki, this Medieval mission is a mystery!"

Chapter Six
SECRET PASSAGES

Gustavo found a stable boy to take care of Tiber. The tournament was in full swing, so this was their chance to get to the bottom of the mystery.

He and Kiki made their way back to the corridor outside the Prince's room, where they'd seen the Horned Knight. It was gloomy, so they were glad for the flaming torches that cast light every now and then.

"How did the Horned Knight disappear?" Gustavo wondered. "There are no doors in the corridor—just three alcoves. There's one at each end and one in the middle, and they are too small for him to hide in."

"He's not a real ghost, so he didn't walk through walls," said Kiki. "Wait here."

She ran back and grabbed a candle from a shelf. "I saw this when we came in," she said. Then she paused. "Oh no—there aren't any matches. We can't light it."

Gustavo grinned and pointed to the blazing torch behind Kiki.

She laughed and lit the candle. It burned steadily but, as they passed the middle alcove, it fluttered. Then it burned steadily again.

"Aha!" said Kiki. "There must be a draft somewhere." She walked back past the alcove. The candle fluttered again.

"You're right," said Gustavo. "There must be a secret way out. That's how the Horned Knight disappeared!"

Kiki said thoughtfully, "If there's a secret door, there must be a way to open it. The other alcoves have plain stone borders, but this one's carved with bunches of grapes. Maybe one of them is a door handle..."

She ran her hand over the stone carvings.

"Nothing," she said. "Wait—there's a single grape beside this bunch."

She pressed it. Nothing happened.

"It's hopeless," Gustavo said. "There's no secret door."

But Kiki peered closely at the carving. "I think that grape is part of a door latch."

She tried twisting it. Then she grasped it firmly and pulled. Gustavo heard metal scraping.

"Keep pulling!" he said excitedly.

The grape came away from the stone surrounding it. It was attached to a chain.

"Push the wall!" said Kiki.

The back of the alcove shifted slightly.

"Harder!" she said. "It's moving!"

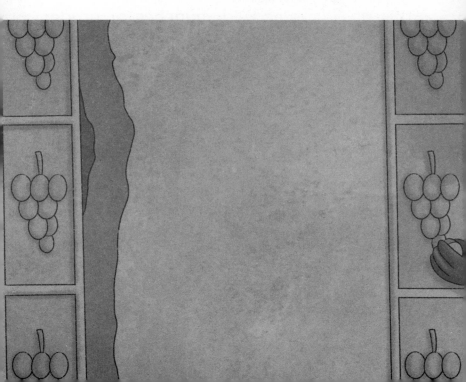

The wall swung open.

Gustavo looked at Kiki admiringly. "How did you do that?"

Kiki smiled back at him. "Simple engineering. The end of the chain lifted a metal bar out of its socket, freeing the secret door."

Gustavo was very glad he had the Engineering Explorer with him. "Awesome! So we know how the Horned Knight vanished. Now let's find out where he went..."

Gustavo lifted a torch from its holder, to light their way. They went down a stone stairway into a dark passage, cut out of rock. There was a damp, musty smell, but Gustavo could feel the movement of air. They soon discovered that there was more than one passage. There were several, which seemed to run under the whole of the castle.

Gustavo was just wishing the Horned Knight had left some more glowing prints for them to follow, when they entered a cavern with a wide, deep hollow in the ground. "It looks as if there was an underground lake here once," Kiki said.

"You're right," said Gustavo. "The water's evaporated and left some white powder behind." He noticed how it sparkled in the torchlight.

"I've seen this before," Kiki said. "It's sodium bicarbonate. It's used in baking to make cakes rise." She glanced around. "There's still no sign of the Horned Knight," she said.

"Not even a footprint," said Gustavo. "Let's move on."

In the next passage, he spotted a dark wooden door, set back in the rocky wall. It opened easily, as if it was well used.

The Explorers went inside and gasped. On the right was a suit of armor, and on the ground beside it was... a horned helmet!

Kiki grabbed Gustavo's sleeve. "Look!" She pointed to some wooden trays filled with small logs. Growing on them were fungi—like mushrooms, but with thin flat tops. And they were glowing green!

Kiki's eyes shined in the torchlight. "The Count used these fungi to make his armor glow!" she said.

"And to make glowing footprints in the crypt!" said Gustavo. "We were right. The haunting does have a logical explanation. Now we—" He stopped. Footsteps sounded from behind the rock wall at the back of the room. He heard clicks and creaks.

"That must be the Count!" whispered Gustavo. "Stand flat against the wall. Let's hope when the door opens it hides us from view."

"Get ready to catch him," said Kiki. "We're about to solve the mystery..."

A section of wall opened inward, like a door. Gustavo heard a rustling sound, like the swishing of silky fabrics.

The door swung wide and the intruder

entered. Gustavo stared in stunned surprise.

There, looking equally shocked, stood...
Countess Cornelia!

Chapter Seven
A PLAN FIT FOR A PRINCE

"You're the Horned Knight?" Gustavo said to Countess Cornelia. "Oh dear!" Cornelia's eyes were wide. "You figured it out. Yes, it was me."

"We thought it was the Count," said Kiki.

"He's too tall for the armor," said the Countess. "It had to be me."

"The gloves under Tiber's saddle were yours!" said Kiki.

"Yes, I snuck into the stables... I didn't mean to scare Tiber so much," said the Countess. "I just wanted to startle him so he'd throw Sir Leonard from the saddle." She sighed. "The Count and I have been trying to make sure Prince Alfred doesn't take the castle. He'd be unkind to our servants, and the peasants who farm our lands. They're good people. They don't deserve that. So we thought that if the Prince believed our castle was haunted, he wouldn't want it. That's why I pretended to be the Horned Knight."

"Did you make the glowing footprints too?" asked Kiki.

The Countess nodded. "I thought if I made ghostly things happen, or weird things like Tiber suddenly throwing Sir Leonard..."

She buried her face in her hands. "But it hasn't worked. Prince Alfred wants the castle more than ever."

"Don't be upset," said Kiki. "What are you planning next?"

The Countess looked miserable. "I don't know," she said. "I don't think I'm very good at secret plans."

Gustavo grinned. "We're quite experienced at secret things, aren't we, Kiki? Er, I mean, Geoffrey."

The Countess looked up. "Geoffrey? But you said Kiki."

Kiki hesitated, then pulled off her hat, letting her hair tumble free.

"You're a girl!" said the Countess.

"I've been pretending to be a boy, just like you've been pretending to be a knight," said Kiki.

The Countess was grinning. "I've always said girls can do anything."

"We're on a mission," Gustavo explained. "A bit like knights on a quest. It's been a mystery so far, but now I know what we've been sent here to do. We're going to make Prince Alfred so scared, he leaves the castle and never comes back!"

After they'd left the underground passages, and said goodbye to Countess Cornelia, Gustavo and Kiki decided to contact the Exploration Station to find out more about the fungi. They'd come up with a plan to scare off Prince Alfred, and hoped to use the fungi as part of it...

They reached the Beagle, which was lined up with some other carts at the side of the courtyard.

BEEP BEEP BEEP! the Beagle said excitedly.

"We missed you, too," said Gustavo, patting the side of the cart. "We need to keep the noise down, though."

"Stay out of view," Kiki whispered, as they climbed onto the Beagle. "We don't want anyone seeing us talking to a cart!"

Once Kiki had pulled a rough sheet of material over them, Gustavo opened the panel that concealed the Beagle's communications equipment.

PEEP!

He giggled. "The Beagle's whispering now, too—it said peep instead of beep!"

"Beagle to Exploration Station," Kiki said quietly. "Beagle to Exploration Station."

The screen crackled. "Exploration Station to Beagle..."An image appeared. It showed six smiling Secret Explorers, crowded around the screen.

"Is everything OK?" asked Connor.

"How's the mission going?" Tamiko wanted to know.

"We'll bring you up to date," said Gustavo. "Or rather, back to date. We're in a Medieval castle!"

He and Kiki filled the Explorers in, then Gustavo showed them the fungus.

Leah the Biology Explorer gave a whoop. "Panellus stipticus!" she said. "That's the Latin name. It's also called 'bitter oyster'. I've never seen one close up. It's bioluminescent—which means it glows!"

"Can you tell us anything about it?" asked Kiki.

"They like to be damp, and they glow in the dark," said Leah. "If you want to use them when it's not completely dark, make sure they're freshly picked."

"Great advice" said Gustavo. "Thank you!"

"Good luck!" cried the other Explorers.

Kiki switched off the communications system. Gustavo grinned. "Let's put our plan into action!"

Chapter Eight
SAVING THE CASTLE

A short while later, Gustavo met Kiki back at the Beagle. He glanced around to make sure no one was watching, and showed her a small sack. "Black powder from the armory," he said, "and some niter. It was easy to get—the only worker there was sleeping in a corner."

"The head cook gave me sugar for my smoke potion," said Kiki. "I told him it was for Cornelia. Then I went back to the underground lake and got some sodium bicarbonate."

Gustavo examined the rest of the goods. "So that's everything except colored dye," he said. "Where could we get that?"

"People dye things in laundries," said Kiki. "Let's ask Margrit the washerwoman."

"Great idea!" said Gustavo. He tucked everything inside the Beagle, out of sight, and followed Kiki to the laundry. She peeked in and beckoned to Margrit, who came outside.

"Yes, lads?" she said curiously.

"Margrit," said Gustavo, "please trust us. We're doing something for the Count and Countess that we believe might make Prince

Alfred go away. We need some colored dye for our plan... Will you help?"

"Of course I will," she said. "Anything to get rid of that nasty Alfred!"

In no time at all, the Explorers were back at the Beagle with everything they needed.

The plan was on!

Gustavo strolled outside Prince Alfred's tower with his small sack of black powder. He piled it near the entrance and slipped inside. Directly above the little heap was a tall, thin window, which he knew was called an arrow loop because archers fired through it to defend the castle. Gustavo peered through it, watching for the Prince and his men.

At last, they appeared. Prince Alfred was pointing around the castle as he walked.

"When I live here, that'll be where I keep my collection of carriages," he said. "And I'll knock down that tower, and build one that's even taller..."

They reached the tower where Gustavo was hiding. He pulled away from the window.

There was a creak as the door opened. Then there were footsteps, and the Prince's voice boomed as they entered the tower.

Here goes! thought Gustavo.

Quickly, he used a torch mounted on the wall to light a rag, and dropped it through the arrow loop. It landed on the heap of black powder, and... **WHOOSH!**

Flames shot into the air in an explosion of blinding light. Clouds of thick smoke billowed around the doorway.

"Help!" Prince Alfred shrieked. "Murder!"

He ran upstairs, shoving Gustavo aside as he passed by. His guards ran up after him.

"I saw the man who did it," Gustavo said to them. "He ran into the crypt!"

The guards yelled, "Thanks!" They thundered back down the stairs and headed toward the chapel, drawing their swords.

Gustavo raced upstairs after the Prince.

The Prince was outside his room, rattling the door handle. "Come on, open!" he was yelling. But the door wouldn't open, and Gustavo knew why—Countess Cornelia had locked it.

Gustavo hid behind a tapestry that hung on the wall. Peering out, he could see Kiki hiding at the other end of the corridor. In her hand was the smoke potion she'd made from their stash of ingredients.

Gustavo nodded at Kiki. She nodded back

and tossed her potion toward Prince Alfred.

It released a cloud of red and purple smoke, which Kiki had made from Margrit's dye.

Prince Alfred shrieked. "Guards!" he yelled. "Where are—"

He stopped as a figure stepped out through the smoke.

CLUMP! CLUMP! CLANG! Countess Cornelia, in her disguise as the Horned Knight, strode toward the Prince. Her silver armor glowed ghostly green, from the fungi Gustavo and Kiki had smeared over it earlier. It was freshly picked, just as Leah had advised them, so it was glowing very brightly.

One glance at the Prince's white face told Gustavo he was absolutely petrified.

"ALFRED!" Count Maximilian's deep voice

roared. He was hidden in the smoke cloud so it sounded like the Horned Knight was speaking. "You must leave this castle NOW, and NEVER set foot within its walls again! Otherwise, you will never escape the curse of the Horned Knight. Do you understand?"

The Prince cowered and nodded.

"SPEAK!" Maximilian bellowed.

"Yes, g-g-ghost," the Prince blubbered. "I understand!" He curled up on the floor, shaking, with his arms over his head.

The Horned Knight backed out through the smoke. While the Prince was still cowering, Gustavo ran after the knight, followed by Kiki. They all hurried to the Count and Countess's private apartment.

Maximilian was grinning. Cornelia took off her helmet, and Gustavo saw she had a huge smile on her face.

Kiki and Gustavo hugged each other. "Mission complete!" said Gustavo.

Everybody in the castle had turned out to watch the Prince leave. He didn't say goodbye to anyone. He pushed a soldier off his horse, leaped into the saddle, galloped through the gate and clattered across the drawbridge.

He was gone.

"Thank you, Gustavo and—er, Geoffrey," said the Countess. She held out a hat. "You dropped this," she whispered to Kiki. "Better put it on."

Kiki stuffed as much of her hair as she could under the hat. "Thanks, Cornelia."

"You are both very brave and smart," the Countess said. "We'll never forget you!" Her eyes twinkled.

The Count nodded. "We'll find you a great knight to serve, and when the time comes, you will be knighted here," he said. "In the meantime..." A servant passed him the Horned Knight's helmet. "This will remind you of how you saved this castle for us." He gave them the helmet. Then he announced to the servants and soldiers, "To celebrate, there will be a great feast—for the whole castle!"

The crowd broke into cheers, but Gustavo and Kiki also heard loud groans coming from the kitchen workers.

"Poor things," said Kiki. "They've got to start cooking all over again!"

Gustavo grinned. "Let's get back to the Beagle before we get roped into helping!"

When everyone had gone to get ready for the feast, the two Explorers climbed onto their cart.

BEEP? the Beagle asked.

"Yes, Beagle," said Gustavo. "Home".

They didn't need a horse this time. The Beagle shot up into the air, and the castle disappeared as blazing white light surrounded them and wind whooshed past their ears. Gustavo and Kiki held tight until the light faded and they were back in the Exploration Station. The Beagle had transformed into a go-kart once more.

Their friends gathered around to congratulate them on another

successful mission for the Secret Explorers. They were thrilled to see the Horned Knight's helmet—which still had some fungus on it, much to Leah's delight. Gustavo carefully placed it on their display shelves.

Soon it was time for everyone to go home—until the next mission!

"Thanks, Kiki," said Gustavo. "I never would have managed without you."

She grinned. "We needed each other," she said. "Bye, Gustavo."

"Bye, everyone!" he said, and walked through the doorway into dazzling light.

When the light faded, Gustavo was back in the Ouro Preto mine. Just as he'd expected, no time at all had passed while he'd been gone, so no one noticed him return.

The strange wailing noises started up again. Adriano grabbed Gustavo's hand and snuggled against him.

"Don't be scared," said Gustavo. "It's just the wind making noises as it blows through twisty tunnels."

"Is it really?" asked Adriano.

Gustavo nodded. "Really. Things

sometimes seem weird, but there's usually an explanation for them. You just need to find the evidence." He smiled, thinking to himself, *There's even an explanation for glowing knights!*

GUSTAVO'S
MISSION NOTES

Running a castle involved a huge list of tasks and jobs. It was vital that everybody kept on top of them if they wanted to keep the nobility happy.

Armorer

The armorer made and maintained the knight's and guard's armor. It was one of the most skilled jobs in any castle.

Rat catcher

Rats were a big problem in castles because they got into the food supply and carried disease.

Cooks

Castle kitchens had to feed a lot of people. There were lots of cooks, such as soup cook, meat cook, and sauce cook. Each one had different responsibilities

THE PEOPLE OF THE MEDIEVAL ERA

Monarch
The emperor, king, or queen had absolute power, and made all the important decisions.

Nobility
Lords, ladies, and other nobles served the ruler. They often lived in castles and had their own servants.

Knights
A knight swore an oath to serve his lord or lady, and could be called on to fight for them.

Craftspeople
These were skilled people who were useful to the nobles. They helped run their castles and make goods such as armor and carts.

Peasants
The majority of people were peasants. Nobles gave peasants farms to work on in return for some of the food they produced.

Chandler
For defense, castles had to have small windows, which meant they were very dark. Other than fireplaces, candles were the only source of light. The chandler was in charge of keeping a steady supply in stock.

ARMOR

Being a knight was dangerous. For protection, they wore a suit of armor. There were several different types, each with their own benefits and flaws.

Plate armor was made from sheets of solid metal that protected the knight from deadly weapons. But the protection came at a cost—a full suit was heavy and hard to move in.

Leather armor

was made from boiled leather that was hardened and shaped. It was more flexible than metal, but it offered less protection.

Chain mail

was made from linked metal rings. It was weaker than plate, but still provided good protection and was easier to move in.

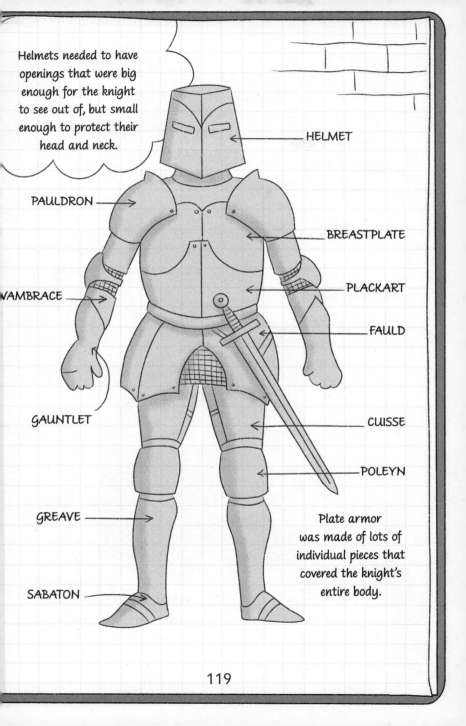

Helmets needed to have openings that were big enough for the knight to see out of, but small enough to protect their head and neck.

HELMET

PAULDRON

BREASTPLATE

VAMBRACE

PLACKART

FAULD

GAUNTLET

CUISSE

POLEYN

GREAVE

Plate armor was made of lots of individual pieces that covered the knight's entire body.

SABATON

119

TOURNAMENTS

Medieval tournaments were the sports matches of the time. Huge crowds of cheering fans gathered to watch knights compete against each other for glory.

JOUSTING

Jousting was often the main event at any tournament. It involved knights on horseback charging at their opponent and trying to knock them off their horse with a lance (a long, wooden pole).

Lances had to be strong enough to knock a knight off a horse, but blunt enough to not cause serious injury.

MELEE

Other than jousting, the biggest event at a tournament was the Melee, which involved knights fighting with clubs, swords, poles, and spears, a bit like gladiators. Sometimes the knights fought in teams, and sometimes they fought individually.

Knights used shields to try to block the lances.

Sometimes the knights competed for prizes, but other times it was just for respect and honor.

Horses were separated by a barrier for safety.

QUIZ

1   Which direction did most Medieval castle stairs turn?

2   True or false: Prince Alfred's champion is named Sir Thomas.

3   What was the name of the horse Kiki and Gustavo took care of?

4   True or false: A knight in training is called a squire.

5   What type of vehicle does the Beagle turn into?

6   True or false: Jousting took place on horseback.

7   What caused the Horned Knight to glow?

Check your answers on page 127

GLOSSARY

ANCESTOR
A family member
who lived long ago.

ARMORY
A place where
weapons were kept.

BATTLEMENTS
A wall along the top
of a castle or tower.

CAPARISON
A cloth covering
for a horse.

CHAMPION
A skilled knight who
jousted for his king.

CHAPEL
A small building used
for religious worship.

COUNT/COUNTESS
A nobleman/woman
in some countries.

CRYPT
A chamber beneath
a church or chapel
containing coffins
and religious relics.

DRAWBRIDGE
A wooden bridge over a moat, that can be pulled up to keep enemies out.

EMPEROR/EMPRESS
A man/woman who rules a group of countries.

EVIDENCE
Facts or information that help to prove something is true.

GILDED
Something that is covered with gold.

JOUST
A competition between knights on horseback.

LANCE
A long weapon used in jousting.

LICHENS
Living things made of fungi and algae.

LIVERY

A uniform worn by the servants of a particular person.

MEDIEVAL ERA

Often called the Middle Ages; a period of history that began in about 500CE and lasted around 1,000 years.

MOAT

A deep wide ditch, usually filled with water, to stop enemies climbing castle walls.

NITER

A mineral used to make fireworks and gunpowder.

NOBLE

A person with a title, such as a lord, count, or princess.

PEASANT

A poor person in the Medieval Era.

PORTCULLIS

A heavy gate that could be lowered very quickly to keep enemies out.

SQUIRE

A boy training to
be a knight.

TABARD

A sleeveless top,
worn by a squire.

ANCESTOR

A jousting
competition.
Sometimes a
ruler would hold
a great tournament
to celebrate
important events.

Quiz answers

1. Clockwise

2. False

3. Tiber

4. True

5. A cart

6. True

7. Bioluminescent
mushrooms

MIX
Paper from
responsible sou
FSC™ C018

For Joe Platt

Text for DK by Working Partners Ltd
9 Kingsway, London WC2B 6XF
With special thanks to Valerie Wilding

Design by Collaborate Ltd
Illustrator Ellie O'Shea
Consultant Anita Ganeri

Acquisitions Editor James Mitchem
Designer Sonny Flynn
US Senior Editor Shannon Beatty
Publishing Coordinator Issy Walsh
Senior Production Editor Nikoleta Parasaki
Production Controller Ena Matagic
Publishing Director Sarah Larter

First American Edition, 2022
Published in the United States by DK Publishing
1450 Broadway, Suite 801, New York, New York 10018

Printed and bound in Great Britain by
Clays Ltd, Elcograf S.p.A.

For the curious
www.dk.com